河北民族师范学院 2019 年度学术著作出版基金资助项目
（项目编号：2019ZZ002）
承德高新技术产业开发区科技计划项目（汇智领创空间专项）：
纳兰诗词影像艺术转化研究成果
（项目编号：HZLC2018007）

康乾避暑山庄

七十二景题诗英译

Poems on the 72 Views of the Summer Resort House
Written by Emperor Kangxi and Qianlong

常亮 译

中央民族大学出版社
China Minzu University Press

图书在版编目（CIP）数据

康乾避暑山庄七十二景题诗英译 / 常亮译著 . —北京：中央民族大学出版社，2021.1

ISBN 978-7-5660-1830-4

Ⅰ . ①康… Ⅱ . ①常… Ⅲ . ①古典诗歌－诗集－中国－清代－英文 Ⅳ . ① I222.749

中国版本图书馆 CIP 数据核字（2020）第 197898 号

康乾避暑山庄七十二景题诗英译

译　者	常　亮
责任编辑	杨爱新
责任校对	肖俊俊
封面设计	舒刚卫
出版发行	中央民族大学出版社

北京市海淀区中关村南大街 27 号　　邮编：100081

电话：（010）68472815（发行部）　　传真：（010）68933757（发行部）

（010）68932218（总编室）　　　　　　（010）68932447（办公室）

经销者	全国各地新华书店
印刷厂	北京鑫宇图源印刷科技有限公司
开　本	787×1092　1/16　印张：15.75
字　数	148 千字
版　次	2021 年 1 月第 1 版　2021 年 1 月第 1 次印刷
书　号	ISBN 978-7-5660-1830-4
定　价	58.00 元

序

"民族有脐带吗？"厄内斯特·盖尔纳（Ernest Gellner，现代民族主义理论家）对此的回答是："有些民族有，有些没有。"研究者更愿用"胎记"（Birthmark）而非"脐带"（Umbilical cord）来表达相关含义。在人类学那里，文化是民族的胎记、遗传的基因。生存环境变迁，政治、经济、科技等造成的不平衡、不均等，使得有的民族连同其胎记湮灭在历史长河之中。相反，有的民族则生生不息，世代赓续，其文化超越民族、种族与国家限域，成为人类共同记忆。当我们把视线集中在17世纪中后期到18世纪中叶的中国，一座距离大清帝国首都京师250公里的皇家园林——避暑山庄（热河行宫）时，此种感觉愈发真切。康熙五十二年（1713）意大利传教士马国贤将康熙避暑山庄三十六景制成铜版画，这些融西方艺术技法与中国古典美学于一体的艺术品受到上流社会追捧，康熙也常用它来赏赐王公大臣，以示恩宠。这些带着中华民族胎记的铜版画被马国贤带回欧洲，触发了欧洲园林艺术乃至美学观念的颠覆性变化，"Sharawadgi"（不规则美）为西方人探索美的建造提供了东方智慧。将这些烙刻着中华文化胎记且已成为共同记忆的艺术呈现给英语世界的人们，就是基于这样的理念：今天人类更需要多元文化，不同文化应相互尊重，用交往、交流和交融来打破隔阂、偏见与歧视。

毕国忠

2020 年 3 月

目 录

康熙避暑山庄三十六景诗英译 / 1

乾隆避暑山庄三十六景诗英译 / 125

Contents

**Emperor Kangxi's 36 Poems Attributed to the 36
Scenery Spots of the Summer Resort House** / 1

Emperor Qianlong's 36 Poems Attributed to the 36 Scenery Spots of the Summer Resort House

康熙避暑山庄三十六景诗英译

Emperor Kangxi's 36 Poems Attributed to the 36 Scenery Spots of the Summer Resort House

烟波致爽

Yan Bo Zhi Shuang (Brisk Breeze Brought by Misty Ripples)

其一　烟波致爽并序

热河地既高敞，气亦清朗，无蒙雾霾氛，柳宗元记所谓旷如也。四围秀岭，十里澄湖，致有爽气。"云山胜地"之南，有屋七楹，遂以"烟波致爽"颜其额焉。

山庄频避暑，静默少喧哗。

北控远烟息，南临近壑嘉。

春归鱼出浪，秋敛雁横沙。

触目皆仙草，迎窗遍药花。

炎风昼致爽，绵雨夜方赊。

土厚登双谷，泉甘剖翠瓜。

古人戍武备，今卒断鸣笳。

生理农商事，聚民至万家。

The 1ˢᵗ View: "Yan Bo Zhi Shuang" (Brisk Breeze Brought by Misty Ripples) with Prologue

Rehe (former name of Chengde) is located in a high and open stretch of land of the Yanshan Mountain area with a moderate climate. The place is rarely enveloped by fog and obscuring haze; and the scenery here resembles what Liu Zongyuan (a Tang Dynasty poet) describes as a "Grand View" in one of his poems. Breeze from the hills and surrounding lakes brings brisk air to the south of "Yun Shan Sheng Di" (The Blessed Lot of Cloud Mountain [View 8]), the setting of a building of seven yards is setting. I (Emperor Kangxi) named it "Yan Bo Zhi Shuang" (Brisk Breeze Brought by Misty Ripples) and inscribed it on the placard of the major hall.

For many times I come to the Mountain Resort to escape the steaming days,

Here is peace and quiet without worldly noise.

The war fire of the northern boundary has ceased,

So I feel free to enjoy the beautiful mountain views here.

Cheerful fish leap from waves when spring returns,

And wild geese fly across deserts in autumn.

Come into my eyes are herbs of longevity,

Outside my windows grow medicinal flowers.

During the daytime I feel the brisk breezes from the north,

At night I hear the sound of drizzling rain.

The double-head grain yields in this fertile land indicates a good harvest,

And the orchards watered by fine springs yield fruits that are so sweat.

Former dynasties guarded this area with armed forces,

Now, the horn of war from soldiers has long been disappeared.

Farmers and merchants have found their ways of good life,

And the number of families gathering here is beyond 10,000.

芝径云堤

Zhi Jing Yun Di (Lingzhi Path on a Dyke to Clouds)

其二　芝径云堤并序

　　夹水为堤，逶迤曲折，径分三枝，列大小洲三，形若芝英，若云朵，复若如意。有二桥通舟楫。

万几少暇出丹阙，乐水乐山好难歇。

避暑漠北土脉肥，访问村老寻石碣。

众云"蒙古牧马场，并乏人家无枯骨。

草木茂，绝蚊蝎，泉水佳，人少疾"。

因而乘骑阅河隈，湾湾曲曲满林樾。

测量荒野阅水平，庄田勿动树勿发。

自然天成地就势，不待人力假虚设。

君不见，磬锤峰，独峙山麓立其东。

又不见，万壑松，偃盖重林造化同。

煦妪光临承露照，青葱色转频岁丰。

游豫常思伤民力，又恐偏劳土木工。

命匠先开芝径堤，随山依水揉辐齐。

司农莫动帑金费，宁拙舍巧洽群黎。

边垣利刃岂可恃，荒淫无道有青史。

知警知戒勉在兹，方能示众抚遐迩。

虽无峻宇有云楼，登临不解几重愁。

连岩绝涧四时景，怜我晚年宵旰忧。

若使扶养留精力，同心治理再精求。

气和重农紫宸志，烽火不烟亿万秋。

The 2nd View "Zhi Jing Yun Di" (Lingzhi [①] Path on a Dyke to Clouds) with Prologue

A dyke stretches its winding way across the lake and its three branches connect three islets with two bridges. The shape of the three islets connected by the dyke resembles that of a Lingzhi, the fairy herb of longevity.

Despite myriad affairs, I found some time to leave the Forbidden City,

So weariness can not stop me to enjoy the view of streams and mountains.

I came to this fertile land to get away from the steaming summer,

And consulted village elders if I would come across some old inscriptions.

They told me "the lands were originally a pasture that was scarcely trodden by people.

---

① Lucid Ganoderma, a rare and fairy herb in Chinese culture that symbolizes longevity.

Trees and grass here grow luxuriantly; mosquitos and scorpions are rarely seen.

Water in the springs here is so fine that the people here rarely suffer from illness".

With the guidance of village elders, I rode off to inspect a river bend.

Twisting and turning, the river went through the shady groves.

Surveyors began their measuring job under my orders,

Without destroying farming land or cutting down any trees.

For the scenery here is so natural, it is free from the labor to build man-made hills

or rivers.

Couldn't you see? With its peculiar shape, Hammer Peak stands to the east.

Couldn't you see? The shades of pine trees cover the myriad vales, so luxuriant.

Nature nurtures all the things and the verdant crops indicate a good harvest.

The building of Mountain Resort offered me a place to entertain and rest,

But I worried that too much labor from the people would be spent.

So I ordered my architects to dig lakes and build embankments and Lingzhi Path ,

With other scenery spots built around the natural mountains and streams.

I also ordered my Chamberlain to use no money from the government treasury.

Because I prefer the rustic rather than luxuriance,

And by this way I wanted to keep accord with my subjects' taste.

The safety of the country could not only be ensured,

By the protection of the Great Wall and armed forces.

As all the historical chronicles record,

It is always the licentiousness of rulers that ruins states.

So I will keep alert and restraint,

Then I can become a model for people from afar and near.

And standing on the high pavilion,

I still felt the worry about country and people.

All around are the beautiful mountains and rivers of four seasons,

And it seems that this fine scenery brings comfort,

To me as an old man who is always occupied by state affairs.

If I have revived my energy after the rest here,

I would select capable men to help me to bring about a better governing of the country.

Because what I care for is to promote farming to bring a better live for the people,

Having a peaceful country and a perpetual governing of the dynasty is always my will.

无暑清凉

Wu Shu Qing Liang (Un-summerly Clear and Cool)

其三　无暑清凉并序

循芝径北行，折而少东，过小山下，红莲满渚，绿树缘堤。西南夏屋轩敞，长廊联络，为"无暑清凉"。山爽朝来，水风微度，泠然善也。

畏景先愁永昼长，晚年好静益彷徨。

三庚退暑清风至，九夏迎凉称物芳。

意惜始终宵旰志，踟蹰自问济时方。

谷神不守还崇政，暂养回心山水庄。

The 3rd View "Wu Shu Qing Liang" (Un-summerly Clear and Cool) with Prologue

Following the "Zhi Jing Yun Di" (Lingzhi Path on a Dyke to Cloud) and heading to the east for a while, passing by a low hill, here you will find red lotus blossoms around the sandbar, and green trees with their shade covering the banks. To the southwest there is a large and open building connected by long corridors. This is "Wu Shu Qing Liang" (Un-summerly Clear and Cool), because morning fresh air comes from the hills and a breeze from the lake brings refreshing so fine to enjoy.

The hot summer bothers me and the long daytime is so weary,

As an old man, I love quietness and feel troubled by the steaming weather.

But here, even in the hottest time of year,

The cool breezes drive away the heat with fragrant air.

Always with the ideal of a good governing of the country,

I get up very early in the morning and stay up late at night.

Always I pace up and down in the halls,

To think about good policies to deal with state affairs.

But I am unwilling to retreat from the crowd to pursue a perpetual life as a Taoist priest,

Because state affairs are my worries.

And after a temporary rest in the mountain resort to refresh my body,

I will get back to my work to govern the country.

延薰山馆

Yan Xun Shan Guan (The Mountain Mansion of Continuous Breeze)

其四　延薰山馆并序

入"无暑清凉"转西，为"延薰山馆"，楹宇守朴，不腝不雕，得山居雅致。启北户，引清风，几忘六月。

夏木阴阴盖溽暑，炎风款款守峰衔。
山中无物能解愠，独有清凉免脱衫。

The 4th View "Yan Xun Shan Guan" (The Mountain Mansion of Continuous Breeze) with Prologue

After entering "Wu Shu Qing Liang" (Un—summerly Clear and Cool) and turning west for a while, you come across a group of building named "Yan Xun Shan Guang" (The Mountain Mansion of Continuous Breeze). The halls here are unadorned and without carvings, paintings and other decorations; they are lovely for their simplicity and elegance. I nearly forget it is the steaming summer of June when a delightful breeze blows in after opening the north window.

The thick shade of the luxuriant trees diminish the heat of summer,

From between the two hills nearby my hall, blows in the north east wind.

In the mountain nothing can release me from the steaming hot better,

Than the cozy breeze that delights me and frees me from taking off my coat.

其五　水芳岩秀并序

　　水清则芳，山静则秀。此地泉甘水清，故择其所宜，邃宇数十间。于焉诵读，几暇静养，可以涤烦，可以悦性，作此自戒始终之意云。

水性杂苦甜，水芳即体厚。

名泉亦多览，未若此为首。

颐卦明口实，得正自养寿。

择地立偃房，根基度长久。

节宣在兹求，勤俭勿落后。

朝窗千岩里，峭壁似天剖。

远托思云汉，怡神至星斗。

精研书家奥，临池愈涩手。

清淡作饮馔，偏心恶旨酒。

读老《无逸》篇，念念祝大有。

水芳岩秀

Shui Fang Yan Xiu (Fragrant Water and Elegant Rocks)

The 5th View "Shui Fang Yan Xiu" (Fragrant Water and Elegant Rocks) with Prologue

The water here is clean and transparent; the rocks here are so elegant. Several dozens of rooms are built here because it is quite delightful to live with sweet spring water. After busy state affairs, I read and rest here to get away from the annoyance and refresh my mind. But I also warn myself not to indulge in enjoyment with this poem.

The taste of water varies with bitterness and sweetness,

But here the spring is so sweet because its source is deep into the earth.

There are so many fine springs with fame, and I have also seen a lot,

When making a comparison, I believe the water here is the best.

It is recorded in the *Book of Changes*,

That only the good choice of food could lead to the longevity.

It's just like the building of a house,

Only a solid foundation could ensure its endurance.

So I should pay attention to curb my emotion and desire,

And adhere to the principle of diligence and simplicity.

Sitting before the window, I behold the view of rocks and ranges.

The most conspicuous cliffs so steep, they must be created by the hands of god, I

guess.

I gaze at the clouds in the heaven so far with these thoughts,

And I feel as if my joyful mind flies up to the starry sky.

Although I study the secrets of calligraphy meticulously,

Sometimes I feel clumsy in my writing practice.

And I prefer a lighter diet than wines however so fine.

I am willing to read the Chapter *Wu Yi* in The *Book of History*,

And wish my country and people to enjoy a good harvest every year.

Note: Chapter *Wu Yi*, a chapter in The Book of History. The title "Wu Yi" means not to indulge in ease
and a comfortable life.

其六　万壑松风并序

在"无暑清凉"之南，据高阜，临深流，长松环翠，壑虚风度，如笙镛迭奏声，不数西湖万松岭也。

偃盖龙鳞万壑青，逶迤芳甸杂云汀。

白华朱萼勉人事，爱敬《南陔》乐正经。

万壑松风

Wan He Song Feng (Pine Vale Villa)

The 6th View "Wan He Song Feng" (Pine Vale Villa) with Prologue

"Wan He Song Feng" (Pine Vale Villa) is located to the south of "Wu Shu Qing Liang" (Un-summerly Clear and Cool), standing on a hill facing the river below. The sound resembles that of reed pipe and bell, when the wind blows over the tall pine trees here. The view here surpasses that of Mgriad Pine Range of West Lake in Hangzhou.

Covering the hills are the pine trees with crowns of canopies and barks, scales of dragons,

Covering the banks are the green lawns with beautiful flowers by the watersides.

White petals and red calyxes touch each other closely, which makes me think of humanity,

And I like the classical teaching in *Nan Gai*, which reminds me of

filial piety.

Note: Nan Gai is a chapter in The *Book of Songs*, the earliest collection of poems in China.

其七　松鹤清越并序

　　进榛子峪，香草遍地，异花缀崖，夹岭虬松苍蔚，鸣鹤飞翔。登蓬瀛，临昆圃，神怡心旷，洵仙人所都、不老之庭也。

寿比青松愿，千龄叶不凋。

铜龙鹤发健，喜动四时调。

松鹤清越

Song He Qing Yue (The Palace of Pine and Crane)

The 7th View "Song He Qing Yue" (The Palace of Pine and Crane) with Prologue

Walking into the zheziyu, here you will find fragrant grass everywhere and rare flowers growing on the high cliffs. Pine trees stand on the hills, and screaming cranes fly in the sky. Here on the mountain, I feel so relaxed and happy as if entering into the fairy lands of the immortals.

I wish my mother a long life,

Like that of green pine trees whose leaves never wither away.

Living here in the palace, she is in quite good health although with white hair,

The four seasons' sceneries are so delightful, and I wish they would entertain my mother.

Note: Pine tree and crane are the symbols of longevity in Chinese culture.

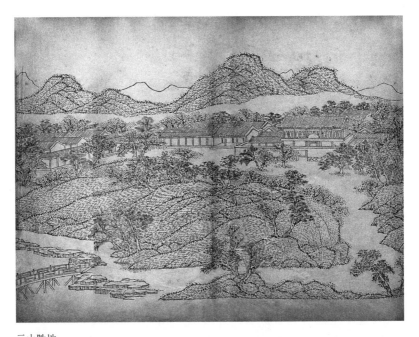

云山胜地

Yun Shan Sheng Di (Cloud and Mountain Pavilion)

其八　云山胜地并序

　　"万壑松风"之西，高楼北向，凭窗远眺，林峦烟水，一望无极，气象万千，洵登临大观也。

万顷园林达远阡，湖光山色入诗笺。

披云见水平清理，未识无惩首节宣。

The 8th View "Yun Shan Sheng Di" (Cloud and Mountain Pavilion) with Prologue

To the west of "Wan He Song Feng" (Pine Vale Villa), there is a high pavilion facing north. Looking out of the window of the pavilion, trees, hills and lakes in the mist are stretching to the horizon. It is really a majestic and grand view.

Looking in the distance from this high pavilion,

I see the landscape stretching to the far away fields,

And I feel that the scenery of lakes and hill are so beautiful,

That it is worth to be written into poems.

When clouds and mists clear away, I see the ripples of lakes,

And begin to understand the reason why the water in the lakes is so quiet and

tranquil.

And I believe if I faithfully stick to the principle of curbing my emotions and

desires,

I would be free from faults in governing the country.

四面云山

Si Mian Yun Shan (Clouds and Peaks on All Sides)

其九 四面云山并序

　　"澄泉绕石"迤西，过泉源，盘冈纡岭。有亭翼然，出众山之巅，诸峰罗列，若揖若拱。天气晴朗，数百里外峦光云影，皆可远瞩。亭中长风四达，伏暑时萧爽如秋。

殊状崔嵬里，兰衢入好诗。

远岑如竞秀，近岭似争奇。

雨过风来紧，山寒花落迟。

亭遥先得月，树密显高枝。

潮平无涌浪，雾净少多歧。

脉脉金明液，溶溶积翠池。

常忧思解愠，乐志余清悲。

素学臣临老，耆年自不知。

The 9th View "Si Mian Yun Shan" (Clouds and Peaks on All Sides) with Prologue

To the west of "Cheng Quan Rao Shi" (White Stone beside Limpid Spring), passing the source of the spring and following the winding path in the mountain, finally there appears a winged pavilion that hovers above surrounding hills. Standing here on a fine day, you can see the peaks and clouds a hundred miles away. When a cool wind blows, you'll forget the heat of steaming summer.

The hills and cliffs and paths are so fine as to be written into poems.

The peaks near and far compete with each other for their sublimity and grandeur.

After an autumn rain, the wind blows hard.

It's cold but somehow flowers here are still flourishing.

The pavilion stands so high and gives the opportunity to see the moon as it first rises,

The trees grow so thick and the top ones are so lofty to see.

The water of lakes faraway is so tranquil without waves,

And there is no fog in the mountain so one will not lose his way among the many

paths.

The worry over my state always drives me to think about,

Policies to free my people from annoyance,

So even in this beautiful scene of mountains, some gentle sorrow still comes to me.

Those knowledgeable ministers around me grow old,

But I am still unaware of my old age because of busy state affairs.

北枕双峰

Bei Zhen Shuang Feng (North Pavilion between Two Peaks)

其十　北枕双峰并序

环山庄皆山也，山形至北尤高。亭之西北，一峰峻出，势陂陀而逶迤者，金山也；其东北，一峰拔起，势雄伟而崒嵂者，黑山也。两峰翼抱，与兹亭相鼎峙焉。

嵚崟冈岫紫宸关，乾地金峰坎黑山。
苦热云生双岭腹，盆倾瞬息落溪湾。

The 10th View "Bei Zhen Shuang Feng" (North Pavilion between Two Peaks) with Prologue

Surrounding the Mountain Resort are all mountains, and the mountains to the north are especially high. One peak with the name Jinshan is to the north-west of the pavilion, and another peak to the north-east is called Heishan. Standing in the pavilion and watching the two peaks, it feels like the pavilion is right between the two.

Two sublime peaks to the north resemble towers out of Palace gate,

The north-west one is Jinshan, and Heishan to the north-east.

The steaming heat of summer is really annoying,

Suddenly I see clouds rise between the two peaks and rain falls at the curve of a stream.

其十一 西岭晨霞并序

　　杰阁凌波，轩窗四出，朝霞初焕，林影错绣，西山丽景，入几案间。始登阁，若履平地，忽缘梯而降，方知上下楼也。

雨歇更阑斗柄东，成霞聚散四方风。

时光岂在凌云句，寡过清谈宜守中。

西岭晨霞

Xi Ling Chen Xia (Morning Clouds over Western Ridge)

The 11th View "Xi Ling Chen Xia" (Morning Clouds over Western Ridge) with Prologue

This building is a two-story tower by the waterside. Sitting here and looking out of the windows to the west, one can see the beautiful glow of the rising sun and the shadows of the flourishing trees.

A rain stops at daybreak, the handle of the Big Dipper points to the east,

Morning clouds in the sky, blown by winds from all directions, change into various shapes.

The beautiful scenery changes as time goes by and there is no need to exaggerate,

I should also keep what is in the heart and avoid meaningless talks.

锤峰落照

Chui Feng Luo Zhao (Sunset View of Hammer Peak)

其十二 锤峰落照并序

平冈之上，敞亭东向，诸峰横列于前。夕阳西映，红紫万状，似展黄公望《浮岚暖翠》图。有山矗然倚天，特作金碧色者，磬锤峰也。

纵目湖山千载留，白云枕涧报深秋。

巉岩自有争佳处，未若此峰景最幽。

The 12th View "Chui Feng Luo Zhao" (Sunset View of Hammer Peak) with Prologue

Standing on this wide pavilion on a hill and watching to the east, one can see many peaks. When the sun is setting and all the colors dye the landscape, the scenery is like a beautiful painting. Among the peaks to the east, a peak stands upright so spectacularly, it is called Hammer Peak (Qingchui means hammer in Chinese).

A thousand years ago, this spectacular peak had been recorded in historical documents,

With clouds and the mountain streams, together they make a beautiful view of autumn.

Every sublime peak has its specialty to boast of,

But in grandeur, this peak dwarfs all of them.

其十三　南山积雪并序

　　山庄之南，复岭环拱，岭上积雪，经时不消。于北亭遥望，皓洁凝映，晴日朝鲜，琼瑶失素。峨眉、明月、西昆、阆风，差足比拟。

图画难成丘壑容，浓妆淡抹耐寒松。
水心山骨依然在，不改冰霜积雪冬。

南山积雪

Nan Shan Ji Xue (Snow-Capped South Hill)

The 13th View "Nan Shan Ji Xue" (Snow-Capped South Hill) with Prologue

To the south of the Mountain Resort, there is a hill with a pavilion on its top surrounded by mountains. In winter, the hill is always covered by snow that melts very slowly. Standing here in the morning and facing the north pavilion, one will be deeply captivated by the snow that reflects the morning sunlight of a fine day. The scenery here surpasses that of many famous mountains.

It's hard to draw the view here, the hills and valleys, even with supreme skills,

The quality of pines' endurance to coldness is impossible for painting, as well.

Everlasting is the water and mountain's spirits,

Their qualities will never change, no matter ice and snow how chilly.

梨花伴月

Li Hua Ban Yue (Pear Blossoms Accompany Moonlight)

其十四　梨花伴月并序

入梨树峪，过三岔口，循涧西行可里许，依岩架屋，曲廊上下，层阁参差，翠岭作屏。梨花万树，微云淡月时，清景尤绝。

云窗倚石壁，月宇伴梨花。

四季风光丽，千岩土气嘉。

莹情如白日，托志结丹霞。

夜静无人语，朝来对客夸。

The 14th View "Li Hua Ban Yue" (Pear Blossoms Accompany Moonlight) with Prologue

After entering the Pear Tree Valley, passing a fork in the road, and following the course of a brook to the west for about a mile, a courtyard on the slope of mountains is beholden. It has a two–story building with long corridors winding across the hill. When there is a fine night with clouds and the moon shining, myriad pear trees open their petals, the scenery then is very beautiful.

The windows facing the hill are often covered by mist,

The palace in the moonlight, surrounded by blossoms of pear trees is vaguely seen.

Four seasons' scenes here are always so wonderful,

The climate and soil are also suitable for the growth of pear trees and other plants.

White petals of pear trees shine at night like daylight,

Their beauty could be compared with that of the sunset glow.

Such quiet nights I have no audience to relate my feelings,

I am eager to talk to my guests about it the next morning.

曲水荷香

Qu Shui He Xiang (Lotus Fragrance over Winding Stream)

其十五　曲水荷香并序

　　碧溪清浅，随石盘折，流为小池。藕花无数，绿叶高低，每新雨初过，平堤水足，落红波面，贴贴如泛杯。兰亭觞咏，无此天趣。

荷气参差远益清，兰亭曲水亦虚名。

八珍旨酒前贤戒，空设流觞金玉羹。

The 15th View "Qu Shui He Xiang" (Lotus Fragrance over Winding Stream) with Prologue

A shallow and clear brook winds its course among the rock and finally reaches a pool before the pavilion. Many lotuses grow here in the pool with their leaves high and low swaying in the breeze. After a mild rainfall, the pool is full and falling petals float on the water like little wooden cups. The natural beauty here can be compared with the record of Lanting.

The faint fragrance of lotus, now and then, intoxicates people far and near,

The scenery described in Lanting could hardly be compared with that here.

Ancient sages persuade us to keep away from precious food and wine,

And for me, they are not a substitute for the natural beauty that is so dear.

Note: Lanting is a collection of poems written by the poets of Eastern Jin dynasty, among the poets the most famous one is Wang Xizhi, the greatest calligrapher in China's history.

风泉清听

Feng Quan Qing Ting (Clear Sounds of a Spring in Breeze)

其十六 风泉清听并序

两峰之间，流泉濊濊，微风披拂，滴石作琴筑音，与鹤鸣松韵相应。泉味甘馨，怡神养寿，恰合章孝标《松下泉》诗："注瓶云母滑，漱齿茯苓香。"

瑶池芝殿老莱心，涌出新泉万籁吟。
芳槛倚栏蒸灵液，南山近指奏清音。

The 16th View "Feng Quan Qing Ting" (Clear Sounds of a Spring in Breeze) with Prologue

In the valley between two peaks, there is a tinkling spring. The drops of water fall on rocks and make a sound resembling that of musical instruments and echoing the cry of cranes and the sound of swaying pine in the wind. The water of this spring is sweet to taste and good for one's health.

In this garden I can collect fairy herbs for the health of my mother,

The tinkle of spring echoes sounds of nature like a touching song.

Leaning against the rail, I watch the ripples and smell the fragrance of water,

The southern hill, so near, seems to be filled by the melodious music.

其十七　濠濮间想并序

　　清流素练，绿岫长林，好鸟枝头，游鱼波际，无非天适。会心处在《南华·秋水》矣。

茂林临止水，间想托身安。

飞跃禽鱼静，神情欲状难。

濠濮间想

Hao Pu Jian Xiang (Pastoral Dream over Water)

The 17th View "Hao Pu Jian Xiang" (Pastoral Dream over Water) with Prologue

The lake is so quiet. The hills with dense forest are so green. Standing on this small pavilion, watching the swimming fish and listening to the chirps of birds, the view here makes me think about the chapter of *Autumn* in *Zhuangzi*.

Walking by the dense forest and the lake so quiet,

I am so filled with contentment.

The flying birds and springing fish are so free,

That it is difficult to describe in language for me.

天宇咸畅

Tian Yu Xian Chang (Grand View on Sky)

其十八　天宇咸畅（调《万斯年曲》）并序

　　湖中一山突兀，顶有平台，架屋三楹，北即上帝阁也。仰接层霄，俯临碧水，如登妙高峰上。北固烟云，海门风月，皆归一览。

通阁断霞应卜居，人烟不到丽晴虚。云叶淡巧万峰明，雁初过，宾鸿侣。欧雨秋花遍洲屿。

The 18th View "Tian Yu Xian Chang" (Grand View on Sky) with Prologue

In Clear lake, there is a hill that stands aloft. On its top, there are three houses and the one to the north is Immortal's Pavilion. Standing here looking up at the sky above and the lake below, the experience of visiting Miaogao Peak comes to my mind. When I was on the top of Miaogao Peak, the view of Beigu and Haimen was wholly within my eyesight.

The high pavilion surrounded by clouds is so magnificent a place to dwell,

The day is so fine, and here it is so quiet with people's traces scarcely seen.

Clouds vary their shape; myriad peaks in sunshine are so loft,

Geese fly here in autumn followed by swans.

After a mild rain, gulls dance amidst the wind with the falling petals of autumn.

其十九　暖溜暄波并序

　　曲水之南，过小阜，有水自宫墙外流入，盖汤泉余波也。喷薄直下，层石齿齿，如漱玉液，飞珠溅沫，犹带云蒸霞蔚之势。

水源暖溜辄蠲疴，涌出阴阳涤荡多。

怀保分流无远近，穷檐尽颂自然歌。

暖溜暄波

Nuan Liu Xuan Bo (Warm Water with Balmy Ripples)

The 19th View "Nuan Liu Xuan Bo" (Warm Water with Balmy Ripples) with Prologue

To the south of the Pavilion of Lotus Fragrance over Winding Water, there is a small mound besides which a stream ran from the outside of the wall of the Mountain Resort. The stream is a branch of the Hot Spring. Water of the stream washes the rocks here, dense mist surges and makes a significant sight.

The warm water that has its source in the hot spring has the function of curing illness,

For the sprout here is so clean that it washes off all dirtiness.

It seems that the stream is so kind to protect the people the region far and near,

And the poor people are also grateful to what benevolent nature has given.

泉源石壁

Quan Yuan Shi Bi (Springs Dripping from a Cliff)

其二十　泉源石壁并序

　　狮径之北，冈岭蜿蜒数十里，翠崖如壁。下映流泉，泉水静深。寻源徙倚，咏朱子"问渠哪得清如许，为有源头活水来"之句，悠然有会。

水源依石壁，杂沓至河隈。

清镜分霄汉，层波溅碧苔。

日长定九数，发白考三才。

天贶名犹鄙，居心思道该。

The 20th View "Quan Yuan Shi Bi" (Springs Dripping from a Cliff) with Prologue

Following the royal road northward, here hills and mountains stretch for miles, and the cliff stands vertically like a wall. At its foot, there is a spring so quiet and so deep. While walking along its course to probe its source, I recite Zhuxi's famous sentence "How can the stream be so clear? Because it has flowing water as its source", and begin to achieve a deeper understanding of it.

The source of the spring is found among the rocks,

Where countless tiny streams run into it and the water finally reaches a bay.

The surface of the pool is as clean as a mirror reflecting the clouds in the sky,

The waves raised by wind splash on the mosses on the banks.

The daytime in summer is so long that I have enough time to spend on mathematics,

Although with gray hair, I still spend time on classics and philosophical thinking.

The idea that a country's prosperity is owed to the blessings of heaven is shallow,

Because the management of a nation needs lots of careful planning and meditation.

青枫绿屿

Qing Feng Lv Yu (Lush Maple on Verdant Hill)

其二十一　青枫绿屿并序

　　北岭多枫，叶茂而美荫，其色油然，不减梧桐芭蕉也。疏窗掩映，虚凉自生。萝茑交枝，垂挂崖畔。"水似青萝带，山如碧玉簪。"奇境在户牖间矣。

石蹬高盘处，青枫引物华。

闻声知树密，见景绝纷哗。

绿屿临窗牖，晴云趁绮霞。

忘言清净意，频望群生嘉。

The 21st View "Qing Feng Lv Yu" (Lush Maple on Verdant Hill) with Prologue

Many maple trees are planted on the northern hill in the Mountain Resort. With the lush leaves and dense shade, their fine verdure is superior to that of plane trees and broad−leafed plantains. Standing beside the open windows, enjoying the cool wind and the view of green creepers hanging on the cliffs, watching the landscape below, I feel as if in a poem with such a description: "water are the belts of vine, and mountains the green jade hairpin."

The stone steps bring me on my way to the top of a hill,

Here I reach a villa with maple trees, surrounded by the finest view of nature.

Wind from woods reminds me of the density of trees,

The forest before my eyes isolates me form the noisy outside world.

Outside my windows, hills are like green islets on a sea of cloud,

And the clouds in the sky are as if chasing the twilight of sunset.

I could not express the delight in such a quiet place,

Only wish all life in nature to have a better growth.

莺啭乔木

Ying Zhuan Qiao Mu (Orioles Warbling in Arbores)

其二十二　莺啭乔木并序

《甫田丛樾》之西，夏木千章，浓阴数里，晨曦始旭，宿露未晞，黄鸟好音，与薰风相和，流声逸韵，山中一部笙簧也。

昨日闻莺鸣柳树，今朝阅马至崇杠。

朱英紫脱平原绿，月驷云骊错落骦。

The 22nd View "Ying Zhuan Qiao Mu" (Orioles Warbling in Arbores) with Prologue

To the west of "Fu Tian Cong Yue" (Melon Field beside Shady Groves), myriad tall trees stand here with their dense shade covering a large area of about several acres. When the steps of dawn draw near, and the dew is still fragrant on the leaves of grass, the song of orioles is in tune with the warm wind. Such melodies of rhymes are the musical chapters in the mountains.

Yesterday I listened to the song of orioles under the shadow of willow trees,

Today I stand below the baldachin to see the training of horses.

All kinds of wild flowers are growing on the green pasture,

All kinds of nice horses are gathered here in motley.

其二十三　香远益清（调《柳梢青》）并序

　　曲水之东，开凉轩，前后临池，中植重台、千叶诸名种，翠盖凌波，朱房含露。流风冉冉，芳气竟谷。

出水涟漪，香清益远，不染偏奇。

沙漠龙堆，青湖芳草，疑是谁知？

移根各地参差，归何处？那分公私。

楼起千层，荷占数顷，炎景相宜。

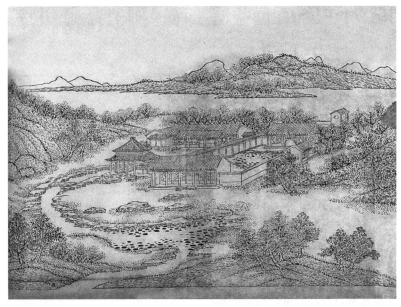

香远益清

Xiang Yuan Yi Qing (Pure Fragrance Spreading Afar)

The 23rd View "Xiang Yuan Yi Qing" (Pure Fragrance Spreading Afar) with Prologue

To the east of Clear Lake, there is a group of buildings with many courtyards. To the north and south of the buildings, many precious lotuses are planted with their large green leaves above the water and red petals covered with morning dew. When a breeze blows, their fragrance can be smelt in the whole neighboring valley.

Standing in the ripples of the lake, the fragrant lotuses are so straight and clean.

Though different in smell, they are difficult to differentiate from each other.

Migrated from other places, they grow well in the Mountain Resort.

With their large flower and petals, they cover such a large area in the lakes,

Their red flowers and green leaves are the best to be appreciated in summer.

金莲映日

Jin Lian Ying Ri (Golden Flowers Reflecting the Sun)

其二十四　金莲映日并序

　　广庭数亩，植金莲花万本，枝叶高挺，花面圆径二寸余，日光照射，精彩焕目。登楼下视，直作黄金布地观。

正色山川秀，金莲出五台。

塞北无梅竹，炎天映日开。

The 24th View "Jin Lian Ying Ri" (Golden Flowers Reflecting the Sun) with Prologue

More than 10,000 plants of trollflower are grown here in this large court of several acres. These herbal plants stand fairly straight with their flowers about 2 inches in diameter. Standing on a pavilion and looking down, the shining trollflowers reflect the sunlight as if gold that paves the whole ground.

The trollflowers here are migrated from Wutai Mountain,

Their pure golden color adds extra beauty to the scenery in Mountain Resort.

Though here are not plums and bamboos in the north of the Great Wall,

The trollflower that flourishes are also worthy of praise.

其二十五　远近泉声并序

　　北为趵突泉，涌也鬐沸；西为瀑布，银河倒泻。晶帘映崖，微风斜卷，珠玑散空。前后池塘，白莲万朵，花芬泉响，直入庐山胜境矣。

引泉开瀑布，迸水起飞珠。
锵玉云岩应，色空有若无。

远近泉声

Yuan Jin Quan Sheng (Sounds of the Spring Far and Near)

The 25th View "Yuan Jin Quan Sheng" (Sounds of the Spring Far and Near) with Prologue

To the north of the pavilion, there is a spring that bubbles up like boiling water; to the west there is a waterfall running down from a cliff like a crystal curtain. When a breeze blows, the splashing water breaks on rocks like pearls flying in the air. To the back and front of the pavilion, there are two ponds planted with lotus. The white lotus flowers send out their fragrance in the sound of waterfall, the scenery here can be compared with that of Lushan Mountain.

The spring runs down from the hill and makes a fall,

The splashing water slaps rocks and breaks into flying pearls.

Standing near, the sound is so delightful, just like the sound of jades hitting each other,

Standing far away, the sound is so faint and echoes in the mountains.

云帆月舫

Yun Fan Yue Fang (Moon Boat with Cloud Sails)

其二十六　云帆月舫（调《太平时》）并序

临水仿舟形为阁，广一室，袤数倍之。周以石栏，疏窗掩映，宛如驾轻云、浮明月。上有楼，可登眺，亦如舵楼也。

阁影凌波不动涛，接灵鳌。

蓬莱别殿挂云霄，粲挥毫。

四季风光总无竭，卧闻箫。

后乐先忧薰弦意，蕴羲爻。

The 26th View "Yun Fan Yue Fang" (Moon Boat with Cloud Sails) with Prologue

This pavilion by the lake has the shape of a boat that equals about one room's space in width and several rooms'space in length. It has stone rails on both sides and several windows. Standing on the upper floor of the pavilion and looking afar, I feel just like drifting like a cloud and floating beside the moon.

Floating on the water without disturbing the surface to wave,

This pavilion is likely to be carried on the back of a sacred turtle.

It is also like a fairy palace in Penglai,

Or a shining picture hanging in the sky.

The sceneries of the four seasons here are always so beautiful,

Lying in the pavilion, the sound of water is as sweet as a melody.

But I will never stop anticipating of the people and relaxing after them,

This spirit is contained in The *Book of Change* and in accordance with that of Fu

Hsi paint Bagua who served their people full heartedly.

Note: Yao and Shun are two great legendary emperors in ancient China.

芳渚临流
Fang Zhu Lin Liu (A Fragrant Islet by Flowing Water)

其二十七　芳渚临流并序

　　亭临曲渚，巨石枕流，湖水自长桥泻出，至此折而南行。亭左右，岸石天成，亘二里许，苍苔紫藓，丰草灌木，极似范宽图画。

堤柳汀沙翡翠茵，清流芳渚跃凡鳞。

数丛夹岸山花放，独坐临流惜谷神。

The 27th View "Fang Zhu Lin Liu" (A Fragrant Islet by Flowing Water) with Prologue

Here is a pavilion above the winding water that runs over large rocks. The lake water runs down under a long bridge, and turns southward here. The banks on both sides of the pavilion are decorated with natural rocks and stretch for more than two miles. Along the banks there are mosses and lush bushes. The scenery here highly resembles the landscape paintings of Fan Kuan, a famous painter in Song dynasty.

Green willow trees stretch their long branches over long bank and islet,

Fresh grass is like a large carpet that is so smooth.

Clusters of mountain flowers by the lake are flourishing,

Sitting here in the pavilion, I feel the quiet environment is benefit to my health.

其二十八　云容水态并序

　　关口之南，有室东向，缘坡下望，绿树为田，青峰如堵，川流溶溶，白云冶冶，不知孰为云，孰为水也。由长桥而渡，疑入四明山中，一径分过云南北。

雨过云容易散，波流水态长存。
悠然世俗为念，必得经书考原。

云容水态

Yun Rong Shui Tai (Shapes of Cloud and Looks of Water)

The 28th View "Yun Rong Shui Tai" (Shapes of Cloud and Looks of Water) with Prologue

To the south of the mountain pass in Pine and Cloud Valley, there is a pavilion on the hill slope facing eastward. Looking down from the pavilion, one can see green mountains and trees, running rivers and clouds that change their shapes. Crossing a bridge and entering the mountain, there is a track that divides north and south.

The clouds in the sky are likely to disperse after a fall of rain,

The water with ripples is likely to retain its quietness.

To understand nature deeply,

One should study the classics thoroughly and apply the rules.

澄泉绕石

Cheng Quan Rao Shi (White Stone beside Limpid Spring)

其二十九　澄泉绕石并序

　　亭南临石池，西二里许为泉源。源自石罅出，截架鸣筒，依山引流，曲折而至。雨后溪壑奔注，各作石堰以遏泥沙，故池水常澄澈可鉴。

每存高静意，至此结衡茅。

树密开行路，山长疑近邻。

水泉绕旧石，雊雀乐新巢。

晴夜荷珠滴，露凝众木梢。

The 29th View "Cheng Quan Rao Shi" (White Stone beside Limpid Spring) with Prologue

To the south of the pavilion there is a pond surrounded by rocks. Walking westward for about 2 miles, one can see the source of the water of the pond. The water runs out from cracks in rocks, and runs through the winding course of bamboo tubes into the pond mentioned above. A stone bank is built to stop the mud and sand brought by floods after heavy rainfall, so the water in the pond is always clear and limpid.

I always pursue a quiet and transcendental state of mind,

So I have this pavilion built here as a place for my meditation.

Tracks are among the lush woods, and the long winding ranges indicate that remote place.

Stream runs through the ancient rocks, and stray birds sing merrily for their new nest.

Dew drops down from the lotus on fine nights,

And dew drops shine on the leaves of green trees.

澄波叠翠

Cheng Bo Die Cui (Lucid Ripples and Superposed Greenery)

其三十　澄波叠翠并序

　　如意洲之后，小亭临湖，湖水清涟澈底。北面层峦重掩，云簇涛涌，特开屏障。扁舟过此，辄为流连，正如韦应物诗云："碧泉交幽绝，赏爱未能去。"

叠翠耸千仞，澄波属紫文。

鉴开倒影列，反照共氤氲。

The 30th View "ChengBo Die Cui" (Lucid Ripples and Superposed Greenery) with Prologue

To the north of Ruyi Islet, there is a small pavilion facing the transparent lake water. The green mountains, white clouds and lush trees cast their reflections on the surface of the lake. It's a good place for passing boats to moor.

The myriad green mountains stand so loftily,

Casting their reflections on the lake that is as smooth as the surface of a mirror.

The purple light glitters on ripples,

At sunset the rising mist reflects twilight better.

其三十一　石矶观鱼并序

　　"远近泉声"而南，渡石步，有亭东向，倚山临溪，溪水清澈，修鳞衔尾，荇藻交枝，历历可数。溪边有平石，可坐以垂钓。

唱晚渔歌傍石矶，空中任鸟带云飞。

羡鱼结网何须计，备有长竿坠钓肥。

石矶观鱼

Shi Ji Guan Yu (Watching Fish from a Waterside Rock)

The 31st View "Shi Ji Guan Yu" (Watching Fish from a Waterside Rock) with Prologue

Following a stone-paved track southward from the pavilion of "Yuan Jin Quan Sheng" (Sounds of the Spring Far and Near), one will see a pavilion facing east with a hill at its back. The brook beside the pavilion is very clear with water plants and swimming fish in it. One can do some angling from a huge stone here.

Faintly I hear the fishing songs at the sunset,

Raising my head, I see birds fly merrily in the sky amidst the clouds.

It is no use to admire fish by the waterside,

And it's better to prepare a fishing pole to do some angling.

镜水云岑

Jing Shui Yun Cen (Mirror-like Water Reflecting Clouds and Peaks)

其三十二　镜水云岑并序

后楹依岭，三面临湖，廊庑周遮，随山高下，波光岚影，变化烟云，佳景无边，令人应接不暇。

层崖千尺危嶂，涵渌几重碧潭。

狮径盘旋道北，松枝宛转山南。

沉吟力尽难得，悬象俯察仰参。

至理莫求别枝，经书自有包函。

The 32nd View "Jing Shui Yun Cen" (Mirror-like Water Reflecting Clouds and Peaks) with Prologue

This court faces water to three sides and a mountain to the back. Houses and corridors stretch up and along with the geographical features of mountain. Waves of the lake below and reflections of mountains together form wonderful scenery.

Mountains and cliffs stand like walls,

The green water of lakes seems so deep.

Looking afar to the northwestern slope, one can see the winding royal road,

The pine trees on the south hills stretch their branches so green.

The only thing I do in the nature is meditate,

The secrets from heaven can only be achieved by observation and analysis.

The ultimate truth is hard to be gotten to,

The only way to get to it is to study the classics that contain all the knowledge.

其三十三　双湖夹镜并序

山中诸泉，从板桥流出，汇为一湖，在石桥之右，复从石桥下注，放为大湖。两湖相连，阻以长堤，犹西湖之里外湖也。

连山隔水百泉齐，夹镜平流花雨堤。

非是天然石岸起，何能人力作雕题。

双湖夹镜

Shuang Hu Jia Jing (Double Lakes Resembling Two Mirrors)

The 33rd View "Shuang Hu Jia Jing" (Double Lakes Resembling Two Mirrors) with Prologue

The mountain streams have been blocked by a stone dam here, and a lake to the right has been formed by the water that runs through the cracks of the dam and finally reaches a larger lake to the left side of the dam. The two lakes with the dam between them are like the inner and outer lakes of the West Lake in Hangzhou.

Myriad tiny streams with their flowing water congregate here,

And wind scatters the petals of falling flowers on the dam between two lakes.

If there were not this natural formed stone dam,

How could the bridge be built so wonderfully only by manpower?

长虹饮练

Chang Hong Yin Lian (Long Rainbow Sipping in Silver Water)

其三十四　长虹饮练并序

　　湖光澄碧，一桥卧波，桥南种敖汉荷花万枝，间以内地白莲，锦错霞变，清芬袭人。苏舜钦垂虹桥诗谓如玉宫银界，徒虚语耳。

长虹清径罗层崖，岸柳溪声月照阶。

淑景千林晴日出，禽鸣处处八音谐。

The 34th View "Chang Hong Yin Lian" (Long Rainbow Sipping in Silver Water) with Prologue

A bridge crosses the green waves of the lake. To the south of it, tens of thousands of lotuses transplanted from Inner Mongolia are planted. Among them there are also lotuses transplanted from south China. The red and white petals of lotuses release their fragrance in the wind that reaches far away places.

The long bridge like a rainbow connects hills,

The willow trees and brooks here create a tranquil atmosphere under moonlight.

In fine days the lush bushes so green,

The birds in the woods sing so merrily that their chirping resemble a harmonious melody.

其三十五　甫田丛樾并序

流杯亭之北，瓜圃之西，平原如掌，丰草茂木，麋麚雉兔，交牣其间，秋凉弓劲，合烝徒，行步围，诚猎场选地。

留憩田间乐，旷观恤闾阎。
丛林欣赏处，遍地豫丰占。

甫田丛樾

Fu Tian Cong Yue (Melon Field beside Shady Groves)

The 35th View "Fu Tian Cong Yue" (Melon Field beside Shady Groves) with Prologue

To the north of Cup Floating Pavilion and the west of a melon field, there is a grassland with lush trees and grass. Here wild animals are found everywhere. Carrying my mighty bow and followed by my officers, it's a pleasure to go hunting on foot in this grassland.

Resting in this pavilion and looking at the boundless land,

I dare not forget my people outside the mountain resort.

This place with grass and flowers is such a good place to enjoy the natural view,

The fields far away are seen with well-growing crops indicating a good harvest.

水流云在

Shui Liu Yun Zai (Floating Clouds over Flowing Water)

其三十六　水流云在并序

云无心以出岫,水不舍而长流,造物者之无尽藏也。杜甫诗云"水流心不竞,云在意俱迟",斯言深有体验。

雨后云峰澄,水流远自凝。
岸花催短鬓,高年寸寸增。

The 36ᵗʰ View "Shui Liu YunZai" (Floating Clouds over Flowing Water) with Prologue

The cloud emerges from between the peaks without intent or purpose; the streams run and never cease by day or night. The creation of the Heavens will never stop as the running of the river will never cease. The clouds keep still for only a transient moment and my mind is as quiet as them.

The mountains are so green with freshness after a shower,

The river afar is so quiet as if in stillness.

The flowers by the sides of banks bloom and wane year by year,

And I feel the hair on my temples grow shorter and shorter in my old age.

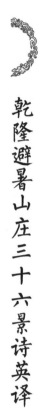

乾隆避暑山庄三十六景诗英译

Emperor Qianlong's 36 Poems Attributed to the 36
Scenery Spots of the Summer Resort House

丽正门

Li Zheng Men Gate

其一 丽正门

行宫因山高下，缭以石城，正南一门曰"丽正"，朝臣启事、外藩入觐，皆由于此。

岩城埤堄固金汤，叆荡门开向午阳。
两字新题标"丽正"，车书恒此会遐方。

The 1ˢᵗ View "Li Zheng Men Gate"

The whole Summer Resort House is encircled by a defensive wall that stretches for many miles. There is a wall due south, through which ministers and chiefs of tribes entered to be received by emperors.

The defensive wall of Summer Resort House with its parapet is stately located and difficult to access.

The major gate opens right to the south with a spacious square before it.

The newly engraved words on the top of the gate read "Li Zheng",

Here the chiefs from tribes far away often enter to pay respect to emperors.

其二　勤政殿

离宫视事之所，颜以"勤政"，皇祖、皇考旧章也。山庄前殿，亦以是名之。

漫施藻棁长阶莎，具足云山四面罗。

不息自强励勤政，永钦家法咏卷阿。

勤政殿

Qin Zheng Dian (The Hull of Diligence in Politics)

The 2nd View "Qin Zheng Dian" (The Hull of Diligence in Politics)

Halls in temporary palaces with the function of dealing with state affairs must have a board inscribed with the words "Qin Zheng" (Be diligent in politics) on it, this is the rule established by Emperor Kangxi and Emperor Yongzheng. The front hall of the Mountain Resort also follows this rule.

The beams and pillars of the hall are decorated with colorful paintings,

Cyperus rotundus grow beside stone steps,

and Mountains afar and hills near are surrounded by mist.

I shall take "the gentleman with virtue" as the maxim to be diligent in politics,

And follow the instruction of the royal family to rule the country well.

松鹤斋

Song He Zhai (Pine and Crane Chamber)

其三　松鹤斋

　　皇太后所御内殿，斋名"松鹤"，祝颐寿也。兹奉圣慈于山庄之东，亦以名斋，随时随地，长乐春晖，用以庆志。

常见青松蟠户外，更欣白鹤舞庭前。

西池自在山庄内，慈豫长承亿万年。

The 3rd View "Song He Zhai" (Pine and Crane Chamber)

This is the residence of the Empress Dowager. The chamber is named "Pine and

Crane" because of the good wish for her to enjoy a long life. It is built in the east

of the Mountain Resort to make it a good place for Empress Dowager to live a

peaceful life in her old age.

It is pleasing to see green pines standing outside the door,

More joyful is the dancing of cranes in the courtyard.

In the Mountain Resort, it is like the fairyland of the Queen Mother of the west,

And I wish my mother live here in happiness and health forever.

其四　如意湖

山庄胜处，正在一湖，堤偃桥横，洲平屿蟲。隐映亭榭，境别景新，此则曲岸若芝英，故以"如意"曰之。

塞水恒流此处渟，柳湖莲岛偶摹形。
烟容波态皆如画，属意悠然在杳冥。

如意湖

Ru Yi Lake

The 4th View "Ru Yi Lake"

The beauty of the Mountain Resort lies in the lake, which is divided by an embankment and bridges. Pavilions are built on the sandbars and islets of the picturesque scenery, and the embankment resembles a Lingzhi (a kind of mushroom taken by Chinese as the symbol of auspiciousness. Jade carved into Linzhi's shape is called Ru Yi), thus the lake is named "Ru Yi".

The water of Wulie River is diverted into the Mountain Resort and merges with springs here to form a quiet lake,

The lake and the Lotus Islet forms the shape of a Ru Yi.

In the suffusing mist and gleaming ripples, the lake is like a painting,

My heart is far reaching like the lake water that stretches to the distant shores.

青雀舫

Qing Que Fang (Blue Bird Boat)

其五　青雀舫

　　澄湖放艇，湖光瑶碧，载月为宜，冲雨亦有奇致。黄龙彩鹢，无取过华。

溶溶塞水浩无涯，桂楫兰桡向晚移。
月朗寥天驾青雀，空明宛是泛瑶池。

The 5th View "Qing Que Fang" (Blue Bird Boat)

It is appealing to have a trip by boat on the wavy lake on a moonlit night, better is to get a rain. The boat is not ostentatiously decorated, only painted with yellow dragon or colorful Yi bird on the prow.

The largamente lake water has no boundary,

Rowing the oars slowly, the boat moves forward in quiet.

With bright moon hanging above the broad sky,

It is quite like I am roaming in a heavenly pond.

其六　绮望楼

楼在城西南隅，下视，缘堤庐阛阓，历历可数。山环水抱，俨在画图中。

埤堄岑楼耸翠林，每因眺远一登临。

"万家烟火随民便"，圣度原如天地心。

绮望楼

Qi Wang Lou (Fair Sight Watching Pavilion)

The 6th View "Qi Wang Lou" (Fair Sight Watching Pavilion)

This pavilion is located in the southwest area of the Mountain Resort. Standing in it, folk dwellings and fairs can be seen. Surrounded by mountains and the river, the scenery is as beautiful as in a painting.

The pavilion stands high among the green mountain woods,

Quite often I stand here and look far into the distance.

My eyes behold the view of the peaceful life of the subjects,

Which is attributed to my Emperor Grandfather's great foresight and meritorious deeds.

驯鹿坡

Xun Lu Po (Deer-Taming Slope)

其七　驯鹿坡

静宜园有驯鹿坡，乃黑龙江将军所进，其地以使鹿为俗。山庄则濯濯麌麌，惟性所适，无异家畜，亦以名坡。

驯鹿亲人似海鸥，丰茸丰草恣呦呦。

灵台曾被文王顾，例视宁同塞上麀。

The 7th View "Xun Lu Po" (Deer-Taming Slope)

In Jing—yi Garden, there is a Deer—Taming Slope. The deer are the tribute of a General of Heilongjiang, where taming deer is a local custom. The Mountain Resort has a good environment for deer to live, and here they are no different from domestic animals. So here the slope is named Deer—Taming Slope.

Here on the slope deer are close as to people as seagulls,

They eat grass and bleat freely on the lush vegetation.

My Emperor Grandfather once watched deer here as King Wen of Zhou did on Deer Terrace,

The tamed deer are for watching but not for the game of hunting.

其八　水心榭

　　界水为堤，跨堤为榭，弥望空碧，仿佛笠泽垂虹。景色明湖，苏、白未得专美。

一缕堤分内外湖，上头轩榭水中图。

因心秋意萧而淡，入月烟光有若无。

水心榭

Shui Xin Xie (Mid-lake Pavilion)

The 8th View "Shui Xin Xie" (Mid-lake Pavilion)

The pavilion is built on an embankment that divides the two lakes. Sitting in the pavilion and looking at the green water and blue sky, one feels like being in the beautiful scenery of Song Jiang's Rainbow Bridge. The beautiful scenery surrounding the stone embankment can be compared to that of Su Causeway and Bai Causeway of the West Lake in Hangzhou.

A long embankment divides the lake into an inner and outer area,

The reflection of the pavilion on the water forms a beautiful picture.

Sitting here, one can enjoy the feel of cozy autumn even in summer,

The glistening light of waves and the faint moon are so enchanting.

颐志堂

Yi zhi Tang (the Hall for Cultivating the Mind)

其九　颐志堂

　　河亭迤北，疏轩面爽，皇祖题曰"颐志堂"。陆士衡有言"颐情志于典坟"，岂徒缮性葆真之为适。

窈窕山深水复清，虚堂夏五足怡情。
欲因致远惟宁静，匪慕嵇康自养生。

The 9th View "Yi zhi Tang" (the Hall for Cultivating the Mind)

To the north of the River Pavilion there is a hall that my Emperor Grandfather named "Yi—zhi Tang" (the Hall for Cultivating the Mind). Lu Shiheng (Lu Ji, 261 —303) said in his work *Wen Fu* that "the reading of ancient classics can cultivate one's mind", but the reading has far more important significance than only to keep one's original mind pure.

The mountain is high and the water is clear,

Sitting in the spacious hall, one can enjoy the mild and beautiful month of May.

What I seek is not Ji Kang's way to keep physical and mental health,

But to cultivate a tranquil mind and lofty morals for the greater good.

Note: Ji kang is a famous literary man and musician in the late Three Kingdom period.

其十　畅远台

清舒山馆之东，临镜湖，为崇台。绿柳遥堤，红荷近渚，墙外群山，罗列奔凑，矫首遐观，斯为最畅。

崇台湖上俯澄清，"畅远"新标即景名。

渊鉴当年超物表，静观万类入空明。

畅远台

Chang Yuan Tai (Distance Looking Terrace)

The 10th View "Chang Yuan Tai" (Distance Looking Terrace)

A high terrace is built by the Mirror Lake and to the east of Qing Shu Shan Guan. This is the best place to look at the green willows and red lotuses by the near causeways and islets and the mountains far outside the walls of the Mountain Resort.

Ascending this terrace one can see the lake and the scenery reflected in it,
Quite recently I named it the "Chang Yuan Tai".
Standing here, I think of my Emperor Grandfather, who recruited scholars to compile numerous classics,
Watching all the things around that have their reflections on the lake, I feel like entering a state of tranquility and clarity.

静好堂

Jing Hao Tang (The Hall of Tranquility and Peace)

其十一　静好堂

　　山庄幽邃，静如太古，盖天地不然。此间竹静苔清，觉鸟语泉声，都增静赏。

翠屏遮户静无尘，馘馘阶前长绿筠。
琴荐笔床都恰当，想因翰墨缅风人。

The 11ᵗʰ View "Jing Hao Tang" (The Hall of Tranquility and Peace)

The Mountain Resort is quiet and secluded, and as tranquil as in ancient time. With fine bamboo and clean moss, here one can listen to the chirping of birds and the sound of the mountain springs that add to the tranquility of the view.

The green mountains are like a screen that cover the front door,

There is no worldly crowd, and fine bamboo grows before the hall.

In the room the mat for playing Guqin and the penholder are properly placed,

The things here recall my memory of my Emperor Grandfather, and I will write these remembrances in lines.

其十二　冷香亭

　　方亭东向，俯临碧沼，荷净蘋香，露白风清时，冰心玉壶，殆不是过。

四柱池亭绕绿荷，冷香雨后袭人多。

七襄可识天孙锦，弥望盈盈接绛河。

冷香亭

Leng Xiang Ting (Lotus Fragrance Pavilion)

The 12th View "Leng Xiang Ting" (Lotus Fragrance Pavilion)

The pavilion to the east of the Square Pavilion and by the lake is a good place to enjoy the fragrance of lotuses. In the autumn season with white dews and cozy wind, one's mind will be purified by the view.

The pavilion is surrounded by green lotus leaves in the lake,

After an autumn rain, the fragrance of lotus flowers is so refreshing.

The lotus flowers are like the colorful brocade woven by Zhi Nu,

Blooming everywhere, it seems that they connect the lake to the Milky Way in the sky.

Note: Zhi Nu is the granddaughter of the Emperor of Heaven in Chinese myths.

采菱渡

Cai Ling Du (Water Chestnut Picking Ferry)

其十三　采菱渡

　　湖波澄碧，水面多菱，叶浮贴水，背日花开，佳实脆香，与莲房、水芝并荐，故取摩诘诗中语名其处。

菱花菱实满池塘，谷口风来拂棹香。
何必江南罗绮月，请看塞北水云乡。

The 13th View "Cai Ling Du" (Water Chestnut Picking Ferry)

Here beside the green ripples of the lake, a lot of water chestnuts grow. Their leaves are close to the surface of the water, and their flowers bloom on the branches. The fruits of water chestnuts are crisp and sweet, together with lotus seedpods and flowers, they form the typical view of the south China water towns.

The flower and fruit of water chestnuts are found everywhere on the lake surface,

The wind from the valley carries the fragrance to my boat.

Why are people sentimentally attached to the view under the south China moon?

Please come to see the scenery in the Mountain resort, it is just as beautiful as there.

其十四　观莲所

　　平湖曲渚，在在荷香，景中以之标名者不一。此间云廊窈窕，方亭虚敞，圣祖题额在焉，洵为甲观。

宝题恒焕圣人字，冰腸仍凭君子花。

助感每教惊逝水，追欢曾未泛流霞。

观莲所

Guan Lian Suo (Lotus Watching Pavilion)

The 14ᵗʰ View "Guan Lian Suo" (Lotus Watching Pavilion)

On the quiet lakes and islets of different sizes and shapes, one can smell the fragrance of lotus flower everywhere. Many spots are named with lotus in the Mountain Resort, they have different features. The quiet corridor and broad square pavilion here make it the best place to enjoy the view of the lotuses, and the inscribed board with My Emperor Grandfather's handwriting is still there.

The inscribed board with My Emperor Grandfather's handwriting has great splendor,
It shines over the Lotus Watching Pavilion that is surrounded by an abundance of lotuses, the gentleman of flowers.
The scenery here often leads me to think about the likeness of flying time and flowing water,
To find joy in nature is what always I enjoy, but I never indulge in the amusement without limits.

清晖亭

Qing Hui Ting (Bright Light Pavilion)

其十五　清晖亭

虚亭临水，清旷绝尘，宵月晨曦，春林秋蓼，扬辉绚目，所谓"清晖娱人"，恍然可遇。

水复山重静且便，奇葩异草四时鲜。

始知谢客饶佳句，拟学唐家度小年。

The 15th View "Qing Hui Ting" (Bright Light Pavilion)

Standing by the water, this pavilion is clean and spacious. Bathed in the gleaming moonlight at night and glistening sunlight at morning, this pavilion is so charming.

Standing among the winding springs and overlapping ranges, this pavilion is quiet and comfortable,

On the ground there are so many flowers and herbs boasting their beauty in all seasons.

Only when sitting in the pavilion, one realizes why Xie Lingyun wrote so many beautiful poems,

Facing the scenery, I want to follow the way of Tang Geng, and spend a good day here as long as a year.

其十六　般若相

　　山庄清净地，有水皆阿耨，无峰非灵鹫。别创兰若，奉妙庄严相，当是踞狮子座说《大般若经》时。

雁堂小筑竺招提，狮子林如画出倪。

无相相中真实相，梵称"般若"岂无稽?

般若相

Bo Re Xiang (The Temple of Prajna Form)

The 16th View "Bo Re Xiang" (The Temple of Prajna Form)

The Mountain Resort is a pure land, the lakes and hills here are like those of a Buddhist

sacred place. My Emperor Grandfather had a temple built on Ru Yi Zhou, where the

statue of Buddha's Dharma body is enshrined. Judging from the posture of the statue, it

should be the Dharma body when Buddha was expounding *The Sutra of Great Prajna*

Paramita on the lion seat.

A Buddhist temple was built in the Mountain Resort, following the custom of

ancient India,

The construction here is like the temple of Ni Zan's painting of Lion Grove Garden.

Buddhism theory believes all things are empty in essence, and Buddha is capable

of the enlightenment of truth in the emptiness,

This wisdom is called "Prajna" in Sanskrit, how could one interpret it as a

fantastical talk?

沧浪屿

Cang Lang Yu (The Islet of Surging Waves)

其十七　沧浪屿

山泉汇为湖沼，澄泓见底，孤屿临流，悠然得沧浪趣。

绿洲朗润蕙兰荣，日对沧浪之水清。

俯洁搴芳无限趣，那更分别足和缨？

The 17th View "Cang Lang Yu" (The Islet of Surging Waves)

The springs in the Mountain Resort converge into lakes, and the water of the lakes are crystal clear. There is an islet in the lake, where one can feel the enjoyment described by ancient songs.

The green islet is bathed in the brightly sunshine, the orchid here is in full bloom,

Everyday, the water of the surging waves are so clear.

There is boundless joy in picking orchid flowers by the clear water,

And one will automatically forget to wash helmet plumes.

其十八　一片云

山中云气，朝暮晴雨，变灭无端。或起树中，或浮水面，或来楼窗几榻间，以片目之，所谓"一滴水知大海味"也。

白云一片才生岫，瞥眼岫云一片成。
变幻千般归静寄，"无心"妙致想泉明。

一片云

Yi Pian Yun (The Theatrical Stage of Cloud)

The 18th View "Yi Pian Yun" (The Theatrical Stage of Cloud)

The fleecy clouds in the mountain are always changing; they vary in shapes at dawn

or dusk. Sometimes they rise from the top of a tree, sometimes they float on the

water surface, and sometimes they even enter the rooms.

A cloud floats out from the valley,

Instantly it turns into a large mass.

The form of cloud is always changing and finally disappears in a secluded place,

It reminds me of "Cloud emerges from between the peaks without purpose" written

by Tao Qian.

蘋香沜

Pin Xiang Pan (The Courtyard of Duckweed Fragrance)

其十九　蘋香沜

　　度桥而北，回望烟水淼弥，碧藻青蘋，溶漾可数。凉风微度，袖拂余馨，何必芳洲杜若。

香风摇荡绿波涵，花正芳时伏数三。
词客关山月休怨，来看塞北有江南。

The 19th View "Pin Xiang Pan" (The Courtyard of Duckweed Fragrance)

To the north of courtyard "Xiang Yuan Yi Qing" (Pure Fragrance Spreading Afar), and crossing a wooden bridge, there is "Pin Xiang Pan" (The Courtyard of Duckweed Fragrance). Here the lake is crystal clear, green algae and duckweed grow in the wide expanse of misty water. When a mild wind comes, it will blow up one's sleeve with the fragrance of duckweed flower.

In the green waves, there is an aroma of water plants carried by the breeze,

In the hot summer weather, there are flowers that give their fragrance.

Lyrists, do not write the line "Spring wind never blows beyond Jade Gate Pass",

To the north of the Great Wall, the scenery is as beautiful as that of south China.

其二十　万树园

　　"北枕双峰"之南，平原径数千余亩，灌树成帷幄，绿草铺茵毯，虽以园名，不施土木。今年都尔伯特部长入觐，即园中张穹幕，集名藩，锡燕、观灯，陈马伎、火戏燕乐之，为时盛事。

"原田每每"曾闻传，"麀鹿麌麌"载咏诗。
秀木佳阴尘不到，乘凉点笔合于斯。

万树园

Wan Shu Yuan (Myriad Tress Garden)

The 20th View "Wan Shu Yuan" (Myriad Trees Garden)

The garden is to the south of "Bei Zhen Shuang Feng" (North Pavilion between Two Peaks), it covers a grassland of about several thousand mu. Having trees as curtains and green grass as carpet, the garden needs not human construction. This year (1754), after the chief of Torghut Mongolia tribe came to pay obedience to the court a great welcoming banquet was held here. Large tents were set up, and bonfires were lighted, equestrian performances and firework displays were held to celebrate the great event.

I use the lines in *The Commentary of Zuo* to describe the plentiful water and lush grass here,

I use the lines in *The Book of Songs* to describe the clusters of deer here.

In the shade of fine trees in the garden that is so spacious,

I find no place that can compare with here to write and to enjoy the cool air.

Note: The Commentary of Zuo, China's first detailed narrative chronicle, is also outstanding historical prose.

其二十一　试马埭

　　我朝马政，超越往代。每当秋狝出塞，考牧别群，相其驽骏，而调试之。故金埒编钱，直是儿戏。

试马榆阴锦埭平，流珠喷玉只虚名。
骊黄牝牡皆形相，骐骥惟当识性情。

试马埭

Shi Ma Dai (Horse Training Ground)

The 21ˢᵗ View "Shi Ma Dai" (Horse Training Ground)

The horse administration of the dynasty is superior to previous ones. Before the hunting in Mulan Paddock, there will be a survey of the pasturing conditions. Horses are classified and examined for their quality, and then they are trained here.

I often watch the training of the horses from under the shade of the green trees on this grassy ground,

The horses well-trained here are even better than the legendary war-steeds.

Horses are not to be judged by their hair color or gender, which are only superficial features,

Only by the survey of temperament and nature, can people find the real quality.

嘉树轩

Jia Shu Xuan (Fine Trees Windowed Veranda)

其二十二　嘉树轩

"万树园"之东，桧栝蔚葱，老干蟠枝，童童垂阴。构轩其下，取无忘封殖之义。

就树构轩阴易得，轩前种树待阴迟。

因知事半功惟倍，契理皆然讵止斯。

The 22nd View "Jia Shu Xuan" (Fine Trees Windowed Veranda)

To the east of "Wan Shu Yuan" (Myriad Trees Garden), there is a grove of cypresses. Their trunks stand upright and their branches stretch to give shade. A windowed veranda was built in the grove in memory of my Emperor Grandfather's fostering me.

To construct verandas near the big trees, one will be able to get shade easily,

If the construction gets erected first and then plant the trees, it will be too late.

From this I understand that to build a house near tree will be effective,

And all things are like that, not only to build a house.

其二十三　乐成阁

　　塞田晚播早收，届白露即已铚艾登场，正秋巡行狝期也。阁踞城墙，垄亩参差，黄云弥望。三时忧悯，于斯稍慰。

远近山田一望弥，秋巡恒值乐成时。

璇题宝篆垂明训，稼穑艰难尚可知。

乐成阁

Le Cheng Ge (Happy Harvest Pavilion)

The 23rd View "Le Cheng Ge" (Happy Harvest Pavilion)

In north China, sowing in spring is very late and the harvest in autumn is early when the white dews fall. It is also the time for hunting in Mulan Paddock. This pavilion is close to the wall of the Mountain Resort, here I can see the crops are ripe for harvest, and the worry in winter, spring and summer is eased.

The fields near and far are all in my eyesight,

The time for hunting each year is also the time for harvest.

The couplets and poems my Emperor Grandfather wrote here are so profound and they should forever be passed down,

And his instruction "to know the hardship of farmers" I will never forget.

宿云檐

Su Yun Yan (Cloud Dwelling Pavilion on Terrace)

其二十四　宿云檐

平台因迥为高，远峙云表，滃浡朝飞，奇峰四起，暝归拥树，萦缭檐端，即景命名，正山中所有也。

出楹写雾还归宿，荟蔚常看颢气通。
却讶稚圭非至此，如何先获我心同。

The 24th View "Su Yun Yan" (Cloud Dwelling Pavilion on Terrace)

This high terrace stands aloft as if it stands above clouds that change form from dawn till sunset. The clouds here float among mountains and embrace trees; the pavilion is thus named to reflect the feature of the scenery here.

Clouds sail out under eaves and among pillars at dawn and return at sunset,

Here one always sees the pervasive cloud covers that bring the fresh air.

The poet Kong Zhigui of the Southern Dynasties had never been here,

But what he wrote thousand years ago in poem, perfectly express my feelings about the scenery.

其二十五　澄观斋

山庄林峦水石，在在仙都，岚翠波光，远近交映，炎歊为之尽涤，足令胸次洒然，岂唯骋怀游目？

背山临水构清斋，翠荫檐端绿绕阶。

别裁不期句成迥，闲居每致意为佳。

澄观斋

Cheng Guan Zhai (Tranquil and Clean Study)

The 25th View "Cheng Guan Zhai" (Tranquil and Clean Study)

The beautiful woods, mountains, water and rocks make the Mountain Resort a fairyland. The green hills and sparkling waves near and far wash away the heat of summer. And this makes me feel free and unfettered, not only when I look into the distance.

This tranquil and clean study is constructed facing water and with green hills at the back,

The verdant shades of trees cover the eaves and the green grass by the stone steps is soft as a carpet.

Only when getting rid of affectation, can one write real profound lines,

And sitting here, frequently fair images of poems come to my mind.

翠云岩

Cui Yun Yan (White Cloud Pavilion)

其二十六　翠云岩

山庄东北多重峦复岭，游云往来，岚翠欲滴，虚檐四眺，正在千岩万壑中。

巉崿横拖一缕斜，浓清细白蔚槎枒。

有形变态无形韵，粉本真堪示画家。

The 26th View "Cui Yun Yan" (White Cloud Pavilion)

The northeast of the Mountain Resort is mountainous. Under the eave of the pavilion and looking out in all directions, one can see the floating clouds go among the green peaks and valleys.

A fleecy cloud floats over the lofty peaks,

The white cloud and green peaks form colorful scenery.

Clouds have shape although it is constantly changing, but its charm is hard to describe in words,

This fine scenery is like an excellent painting, which can be considered as a model to be imitated.

其二十七　罨画窗

横岭如曲屏，"霞标"一室据其胜。前为平台，窗列远岫，题曰"罨画"，董、巨、荆、关，谁能辨此？

霞标云阁小延停，异草仙葩扑鼻馨。

凉峭塞天初过雨，近峰远岭总来青。

罨画窗

Yan Hua Chuang (Variegated-color Painted Veranda)

The 27th View "Yan Hua Chuang" (Variegated-color Painted Veranda)

The horizontal ridge is like a screen, "the Hall of Rosy Cloud" stands in this scenic place. Before the hall there is a veranda, here one can see the mountains far away as in a colorful painting. The name of this veranda is "Yan Hua Chuang" (Variegated-color Painted Veranda), the scenery here can not be reproduced even in the hands of the most talented painters.

Staying here even within a short time,

One can smell the fragrance of exotic flowers and rare herbs.

A rain just falls in the north China sky,

The mountains near and far after washed by rain all appear greener.

凌太虚

Ling Tai Xu (Above Sky Pavilion)

其二十八　凌太虚

　　亭居北岭之复，孤峰拔地，群山环拱。登斯亭者，如陟阆风，俯悬圃，御寇泠然，未足为喻。

冠峰亭子倚嶙嶒，与颢气俱六位乘。
设使步兵曾到此，应闻长啸发孙登。

The 28th View "Ling Tai Xu" (Above Sky Pavilion)

This pavilion is on the highest peak surrounded by hills to the north of the Mountain Resort. Standing in the pavilion, one feels like being in the dwelling of the immortals.

This pavilion stands on the lofty peak,

One feels like riding a dragon and floating in the sky.

If Ruan Ji were here,

He would have heard the shouts of Sun Deng.

Note: Ruan Ji and Sun Deng are famous hermits in the period of Three Kingdoms.

其二十九　千尺雪

　　吴中寒山千尺雪，明处士赵宧光所标目也。南巡过之，爱其清绝，因于近地有泉有石，若西苑、盘山及此，并仿其意而命以斯名，且为四图合贮其地，详具图卷中。

为爱寒山瀑布泉，引流叠石俨神传。
《楞严》蓦地临溪写，离即凭参属偶然。

千尺雪

Qian Chi Xue (Plunging Waterfall Pavilion)

The 29th View "Qian Chi Xue" (Plunging Waterfall Pavilion)

There is a waterfall in the Cold Mountain of Wuzhong, Zhao Yiguang, a hermit of Ming Dynasty, named it "Qian Chi Xue" (Plunging Waterfall Pavilion). I have been there on the trip to south China and was deeply attracted to the scenery there. So in several places that have mountain springs and rocks such as the West Garden in Beijing, the Panshan Mountain and here in the Mountain Resort, I had scenery built imitating that of Wuzhong and named them the same as there. I had also ordered painters to paint four roll of pictures of the scenery of the four places.

For the attraction the waterfall of the Cold Mountain,

I had this similar pavilion built besides the waterfall here.

Looking at the splashing spray, and listening to the sound,

Suddenly I am enlightened to the truth in the *Surangama Sutra*.

宁静斋

Ning Jing Zhai (The Study of Serenity)

其三十　宁静斋

　　诸葛孔明"淡泊""宁静"二语,千古名言。皇祖所至,若御园之"淡宁居"、山庄之"淡泊敬诚",皆取其义。兹以名斋,匪惟慕贤,实以述祖。

既深始静心堪会,致远而宁道亦赅。

妙契神诠参不尽,武侯岂独干时材。

The 30th View "Ning Jing Zhai" (The Study of Serenity)

Zhuge Liang's expounding about "indifference to fame and wealth" and "serenity" has been for myriad years. Both "the Hall of Simple and Serenity" in the Everlasting Spring Garden and "the Hall of Serenity and Reverence" in the Mountain Resort were named for Zhuge's expounding of my Emperor Grandfather. My naming of the study is not in admiration of the prime minister of Shu−Han, but to honor the inheritance of my Emperor Grandfather's instruction.

Deliberateness is the way to cultivate oneself; this is the enlightenment of my heart,

The ideal can be realized only when the mind is serene and concentrated, this truth is complete.

The wonderful expounding of Zhuge is a profound truth that has to be perceived forever,

He had a talent to administer, but was also a philosopher in meditation.

其三十一　玉琴轩

　　"千尺雪"之南，曲涧湍流，潺潺众玉中，韵和宫徵，正不必抚弦动操，已令子期神往。

玉自无言比桃李，水因不竞中宫商。

五言正是薰风节，治慕虞廷化日长。

玉琴轩

Yu Qin Xuan (Jade Lyre Windowed Veranda)

The 31st View "Yu Qin Xuan" (Jade Lyre Windowed Veranda)

To the south of "Qian Chi Xue" (Plunging Waterfall Pavilion), there is a winding mountain spring with splashing water. The sound of it is quite musical, like a tune from a lyre.

The crystal clear spring need not to boast of itself,

Its naturally running water gives a delightful musical sound.

Shun used the words of the Five Virtues to remove the people's worries like the warm south wind,

I admire Shun's virtuous administration and hope to provide the people with peaceful and happy life.

临芳墅

Lin Fang Shu (Fragrance Neighboring Villa)

其三十二　临芳墅

曲阜平冈，缘蹊被隰，无葩不秀，有卉皆芳。别墅数椽，自足幽趣。

奇葩异草四时芬，八百功常鼻观闻。

是药是花皆采取，文殊于此亦疑赝。

The 32nd View "Lin Fang Shu" (Fragrance Neighboring Villa)

Beside the tracks on the undulating hills, many flowers and herbs grow. A villa was built here from which one can enjoy the scenic view and the delight in the peace and elegance.

Flowers and herbs grow here and emit fragrance in all the seasons,

There are myriad merits to smell their aroma.

The flowers and herbs are to be picked indiscriminately no matter if they are medicinal or not,

Because even Bodhisattva Manjusri can not distinguish all of them.

其三十三　知鱼矶

湖水清甘，鱼乐国也。石矶临流，无心垂饵，相忘之适，当非濠上所知。

出水轻鲦乐意洋，临矶欣觉"会心"长。

由来万物天机适，安用劳劳辩惠庄。

知鱼矶

Zhi Yu Ji (The Waterside Pavilion of Angling)

The 33rd View "Zhi Yu Ji" (The Waterside Pavilion of Angling)

The lake water here is clean; it is a paradise for fish. Sitting in the pavilion what I think of is not the delight of angling but the dialogue between Zhuang Zhou and Hui Shi about pleasures of fish.

Watching the fish that jumps out of the lake water onto a rock,

I get a deeper understanding of the philosophical discussion about "the pleasures for fish".

All things become what they are under the rules of nature,

There is no need to discuss "pleasures for fish or not" like Zhuang Zhou and Hui Shi.

湧翠岩

Yong Cui Yan (Emerald Gushing Rock)

其三十四　涌翠岩

石罅泉源出山庄西北，淙淙潺潺，下为瀑布，依岩为佛庐，隔林明殿三楹，东向。晨曦朝爽，空翠四合。

拔地青莲耸德水，天人来往作音娱。

蓦逢杖锡权教往，试问眉毛拖地无？

The 34th View "Yong Cui Yan" (Emerald Gushing Rock)

A spring gushes out from the rock cracks in the northeast of the Mountain Resort. The murmuring water becomes a waterfall. Here a small temple of three rooms facing eastward was built on the rocky hill. The temple is surrounded by hills and woods, in the morning, the air here is very refreshing.

The shape of the rocky hill here is like a lotus flower that protrudes above the water,

The sound of the waterfall here is so loud like that of Buddha's expounding on sutras.

By chance I meet an old monk with a staff in hand,

And I am so glad to stop him for a moment to talk with him about Dharma.

其三十五　素尚斋

　　梨峪清轩，不施雕绘丹雘，皇祖常所御处。崇朴素，明雅尚，备见于天笔标题两字中矣。

弃日无过静读书，读书静合是山居。

披翻却又难耽静，无过明明启迪予。

素尚斋

Su Shang Zhai (The Hall of Simplicity and Elegance)

The 35th View "Su Shang Zhai" (The Hall of Simplicity and Elegance)

In the Pear Flower Valley, this hall has no delicate decorations of colorful painting and carvings. My Emperor Grandfather often stayed here, and his advocating of simplicity and elegance is fully expressed in his handwriting on the inscribed board.

The best way to spend leisure time is to read quietly,

The best way to read quietly is to live in a mountain dwelling.

But when I open books I find it hard to fully indulge in them,

For I am often inspired to think about how to govern the country well.

永恬居

Yong Tian Ju (The Hall of Perpetual Peace)

其三十六　永恬居

　　山中境爽气和，致足怡神悦性。既佳风景，且乐阜安。引养引恬，慎修思永。皇祖御题斋额，意在斯乎？

壶中琼岛郁悬居，景物欢恬气象舒。
已是洞天传玉简，得教福地续琅书。

The 36th View "Yong Tian Ju" (The Hall of Perpetual Peace)

The abode in the hills of the Mountain Resort is cozy and comfortable, and the climate here is also moderate and pleasant. The beautiful scenery together with the peace and prosperity of state gives me ease of mind. To rule the country well, it is important to provide the people with a peaceful life. And I should also cultivate my mind and think about the ways of administration. My Emperor Grandfather named this hall "Yong Tian Ju" (Perpetual Peace), and I guess his intention was the same as mine.

The Mountain Resort is like an Isle in a fairy land, in which a hall lies in the Pear Flower Valley,

The scenery here is so pleasant and makes people feel relaxed and comfortable.

My Emperor Grandfather named 36 scenic spots and his verses on them will be passed on,

I've chosen another 36 and named them my poems, and I hope they may also prevail either.

后　记

　　经过数度的搁置和反复的修改校对，本人的第一本译作《康乾避暑山庄七十二景题诗英译》终于即将付梓。粗略算来，从动笔翻译至今已经将近五年。译者自幼生活在承德这座历史文化名城，避暑山庄各处景点介绍标牌上的康乾二帝诗句有不少是童年时代起就读到过的。后来发现其中有些诗句的英译不是有所缺失就是和原文风马牛不相及，不免感到有些遗憾，这才动了自己译一下的念头。在翻译的过程中，译者常常思考的是如何化解掉原作的晦涩之处，让英语读者尽量体会中国清代两位皇帝面对山庄美景时的所思所想，进而对诗作背后的中华文化有所感悟。必须承认的是，为了实现上述目的，译者在翻译中做了一些简化处理以便于读者理解。至于效果如何，尚有待英文读者的反馈和学界同仁的评价。失误和欠妥的地方是肯定存在的，欢迎同行们批评指正！

　　本书康熙三十六景和乾隆三十六景诗图分别为清代画家沈嵛和钱

维城所绘制。前人余荫，后人感之。在翻译出版的等各个环节，译者有幸获得了许多支持和帮助，首先感谢我的老师曹顺庆教授，感谢您一致以来的引导和鼓励；感谢赵翠华教授在翻译思路和文献资料方面的帮助；感谢毕国忠教授欣然为本书撰写序言；感谢河北民族师范学院科研处和文学与传媒学院少数民族语言文学重点学科研究平台的大力支持；感谢 Margaretha Roos 女士对本书译文的细致入微的校订；在获得作者本人许可的情况下，本书康熙三十六景题诗标题的翻译方式部分地参考了宣立敦（Richard E. Strassburg）教授的研究成果，在此表示真挚的谢意！最后，衷心感谢中央民族大学出版社杨爱新老师、舒刚卫老师、肖俊俊老师出色的编辑、设计和校对工作！

常　亮

2020 年 12 月 15 日